Farmer Joe Goes To The City

Nancy Wilcox Richards

Illustrations by H. Werner Zimmermann

Scholastic
Toronto • Sydney • New York • London • Auckland

For my two-year-old daughter,
Jennifer Elyse,
who already loves to go shopping.

NWR

To Petra,
her patience and her computer.

HWZ

Scholastic Canada Ltd.
175 Hillmount Road, Markham, Ontario L6C 1Z7

Scholastic Inc.
555 Broadway, New York, NY 10012, USA

Scholastic Australia Pty Limited
PO Box 579 Gosford, NSW 2250, Australia

Scholastic New Zealand Limited
Private Bag 94407, Greenmount, Auckland, New Zealand

Scholastic Ltd.
Villiers House, Clarendon Avenue, Leamington Spa,
Warwickshire CV32 5PR, UK

Canadian Cataloguing in Publication Data

Richards, Nancy Wilcox, 1958–
  Farmer Joe goes to the city

Issued also in French under title: Antoine va à la ville.

ISBN 0-590-73361-3

I. Zimmermann, Werner. II. Title.

PS8585.I184F35 1990a   jC813'.54   C89-094973-5

9 8 7 6   Printed in Singapore   04 05 06 07

Farmer Joe lived with his wife
in an old house
in the middle of a big field.

Every day Farmer Joe
worked hard in the field.
He cut the wheat.
He planted the corn.
He pulled the weeds.

But one day he said to himself,
"Tomorrow is my wife's birthday.
I will go to the city and buy her
a present. Something special."

Bumpity-bump-bump-bump
went the truck over the dirt roads.

Clangity-clang-clang-clang
into the busy city.

Farmer Joe was puzzled. There were so many stores! "I need to find something special," he said to himself. "And red, because that's her favorite color."

Cars whizzed this way and that.
Buses zoomed here and there.
Trucks sped up one street
and down another.

Then Farmer Joe saw a big store. A very big store. It was the biggest store he'd ever seen. Farmer Joe parked his truck and went in.

Inside were even more stores.
Shoppers whizzed this way
and that. Escalators zoomed
here and there. Elevators sped
up one floor and down another.

Farmer Joe came to a grocery store.
He picked up a big juicy apple. "It's
red," he thought, "but not very special."

At the next store, he looked at some
shiny red boots. "Not special enough,"
he said.

Farmer Joe went into a clothing store.
Inside he saw some warm underwear.
"These are very red," he said.
"But still not special enough."

Farmer Joe was very sad.

He had whizzed this way and that.

He had zoomed here and there.

He had sped from one store to another.

And he still hadn't found a present
for his wife.

Then Farmer Joe spotted a sign.
It was a red sign.
And it was above a big red store.

Farmer Joe went into the store.

"I'm looking for something red,"
he told the man behind the counter.

"Something special?" asked the salesman.

"Yes!" said Farmer Joe. "Very special."

"How about this?" asked the salesman.

Farmer Joe looked. It was
very red. And he knew right
away that it was very, very
special. "Perfect!" he said.

18

Farmer Joe drove back to his old house
in the middle of his big field.
Past the cars whizzing this way and that.
Past the buses zooming here and there.
Past the trucks speeding up one street
and down another.

Farmer Joe woke up very early the next morning. He cooked a special breakfast for his wife. On the table was the very special present.

Later, Farmer Joe
went out to his field.
He cut the wheat.
He planted the corn.
He pulled the weeds.
He was very happy.

And so was his wife!